Ladybird I'm **Ready...** for Phonics!

Note to parents, carers and teachers

Ladybird I'm Ready for Phonics is a series of phonic reading books that have been carefully written to give gradual, structured practice of the synthetic phonics programme your child is learning at school.

Each book focuses on a set of phonemes (sounds) together with their graphemes (letters). The books also provide practice of common tricky words, such as **the** and **said**, that cannot be sounded out.

The series closely follows the order that your child is taught phonics in school, from initial letter sounds to key phonemes and beyond. It helps to build reading confidence through practice of these phonics building blocks, and reinforces school learning in a fun way.

Ideas for use

- Children learn best when reading is a fun experience. Read the book together and give your child plenty of praise and encouragement.

- Help your child identify and sound out the phonemes (sounds) in any words he is having difficulty reading. Then, blend these sounds together to read the word.

- Talk about the story words, high-frequency words and tricky words at the end of the stories to reinforce learning.

For more information and advice on synthetic phonics and school book banding, visit **www.ladybird.com/phonics**

Book
Band
1

Level 2 builds on the initial letter sounds learnt in Level 1 and focuses on these sounds and their letter representations:

s   a   t   p   i   n

Special features:

repetition of sounds in different words

short sentences with simple language

Is it a tin?

It is Nat.

13

12

Story Words

Can you match these words to the pictures below?

Nat

tin

tap

pin

pan

High-frequency Words

These high-frequency (common) words are in the story you have just read. Can you read them super fast?

is

it

a

16

17

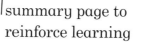

summary page to reinforce learning

Written by Catherine Baker
Illustrated by Chris Jevons

Phonics and Book Banding Consultant: Kate Ruttle

A catalogue record for this book is available from the British Library

Published by Ladybird Books Ltd
80 Strand, London, WC2R 0RL
A Penguin Company

001

ISBN: 978-0-72327-538-1
Printed in China

Ladybird I'm Ready... for Phonics!

Is it Nat?

Is it a pin?

It is Nat.

Is it a pan?

It is Nat.

Is it a tap?

It is Nat.

Is it a tin?

It is Nat.

It **is** Nat.

pan   tin   pin

tap

Nat

15

Story Words

Can you match these words to the pictures below?

Nat

tin

tap

pin

pan

High-frequency Words

These high-frequency (common) words are in the story you have just read. Can you read them super fast?

is

it

a

Ladybird I'm Ready... for Phonics!

Nat Sits

It is Nat.

I sit.

Nat sits.

Nat is in a pan.

Nat is in a tin.

Nat sits in it.

I sit.

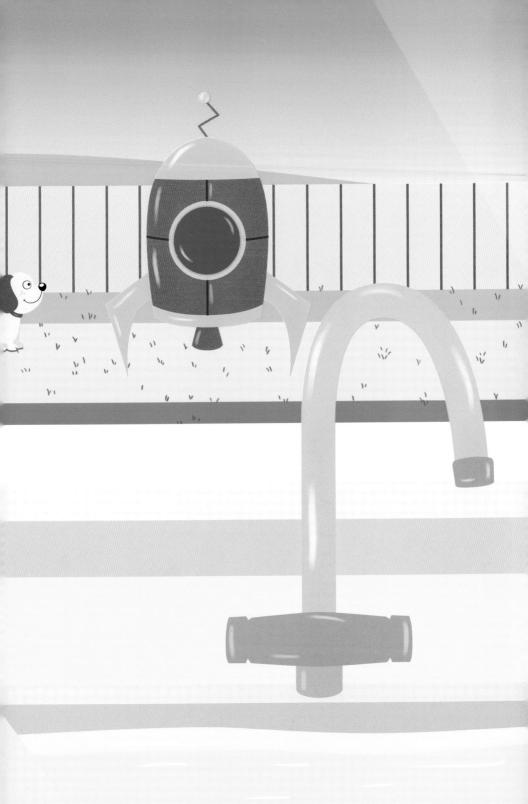

23

An ant.

A tin tips.

It is a tap.

Nat naps!

Story Words

Can you match these words to the pictures below?

Nat

tip

tap

nap

ant

High-frequency Words and Tricky Words

Look at these high-frequency words and the tricky word **I** that are in the story you have just read.* Can you say them aloud super fast?

I   a

is   in

it   an

* High-frequency words are the most common words in the English language. Tricky words are words that cannot be sounded out.

31

Collect all
Ladybird I'm Ready...
for Phonics!

Captain Comet's Space Party

9780723275374

Nat Naps!

9780723275381

Top Dog

9780723275398

Huff! Puff! Run!

9780723275404

Fix It Vets

9780723275411

Dash is Fab!

9780723275428

Say the Sounds

9780723271598

Flashcards

9780723272069

Ladybird I'm Ready for... apps are now available for iPad, iPhone and iPod touch.

Apps also available on Android devices